PARADE DAY

By Judy Kentor Schmauss
Illustrated by Randy Chewning

BARRON'S

Table of Contents

© Copyright 2006 by Barron's Educational Series, Inc.

Illustrations on pages 21–23 created by Carol Stutz

All inquiries should be addressed to:
Barron's Educational Series, Inc.
250 Wireless Boulevard
Hauppauge, New York 11788
www.barronseduc.com

Library of Congress Catalog Card No.: 2005054866

ISBN-13: 978-0-7641-3293-3
ISBN-10: 0-7641-3293-8

Library of Congress Cataloging-in-Publication Data
Schmauss, Judy Kentor.
    Parade day / Judy Kentor Schmauss.
      p. cm. – (Reader's clubhouse)
    Summary: When a little boy is invited to join in a parade, his friends each give him a piece of their costume. Includes fun facts, an activity, and word lists.
      ISBN-13: 978-0-7641-3293-3
      ISBN-10: 0-7641-3293-8
      (1. Parades—Fiction. 2. Costume—Fiction.) I. Title. II. Series.

PZ7.S34736Par 2006
(E)—dc22
                                                                2005054866

Date of manufacture: 09/2009
Manufactured by: Kwong Fat Offset Printing Co., Ltd.
                Dongguan City, China

PRINTED IN CHINA
9 8 7 6 5 4

Dear Parent and Educator,

Welcome to the Barron's Reader's Clubhouse, a series of books that provide a phonics approach to reading.

Phonics is the relationship between letters and sounds. It is a system that teaches children that letters have specific sounds. Level 1 books introduce the short-vowel sounds. Level 2 books progress to the long-vowel sounds. This progression matches how phonics is taught in many classrooms.

Parade Day introduces the long "a" sound. Simple words with this long-vowel sound are called **decodable words.** The child knows how to sound out these words because he or she has learned the sound they include. This story also contains **high-frequency words.** These are common, everyday words that the child learns to read by sight. High-frequency words help ensure fluency and comprehension. **Challenging words** go a little beyond the reading level. The child will identify these words with help from the illustration on the page. All words are listed by their category on page 24.

Here are some coaching and prompting statements you can use to help a young reader read *Parade Day:*

- **On page 6, "Gabe" is a decodable word. Point to the word and say:**

  Read this word. How did you sound the word out? What sounds did it make?

  Note: There are many opportunities to repeat the above instruction throughout the book.

- **On page 4, "parade" is a challenging word. Point to the word and say:**

  Look at the first letter. What sound does it make? (Then cover the *pa* and say:) *Read this part of the word.* (Show the whole word.) *Read the word. How did you know the word? Did you look at the picture? How did it help?*

You'll find more coaching ideas on the Reader's Clubhouse Web site: *www.barronsclubhouse.com*. Reader's Clubhouse is designed to teach and reinforce reading skills in a fun way. We hope you enjoy helping children discover their love of reading!

Sincerely,

Nancy Harris

Nancy Harris
Reading Consultant

I am going to a parade.

It is going to be a
great parade.

I see Gabe.
Gabe has on a black cape.

Gabe looks very brave!

I see Kate.
Kate has paint on her face.

I wave at Kate!

I see Gail.

Gail has a long, long braid.
She has long, long nails!

I see Drake.

Drake has three colors in his hair. They are all shades of blue!

I see Jade.

Jade has a mane and a tail.
Jade is a mare!

Gabe, Kate, Gail, and
Drake stop. So does Jade.

"Come and be in the
parade," they say.

Gabe gives me his cape.
Gail gives me her braid.
Jade gives me her mane.

I am in the parade.
I wave and wave and wave.

Fun Facts About
Parades

- The Rose Bowl is a famous college football game played every year in California. The game is preceded by a huge parade. Every float, or decorated truck, in this parade is covered in flowers, seeds, leaves, or other parts of plants. The average float uses 100,000 flowers!

- When a new president of the United States is elected, the president takes an oath, or promises, to do the job as president. The day is celebrated with a big parade in the capital, Washington, D.C.

- The Olympics are held every four years. Many countries send their best athletes to compete in sports and games. Athletes from all the countries march in a parade as part of the opening ceremonies.

- The Macy's Thanksgiving Day Parade in New York City includes huge balloons in the shapes of cartoon characters. Some are taller than a four-story building!

Chinese New Year Parade Dragon

You will need:

- colored paper
- safety scissors
- crayons
- markers
- glitter
- feathers
- glue or tape
- 2 popsicle sticks

1. Draw the head and tail of a dragon on a piece of paper.

2. Cut out the head and tail of the dragon and decorate them with the crayons, markers, glitter, and feathers.

3. Fold a piece of the paper the long way. Cut the paper along the fold and use one long rectangle for the next step.

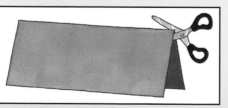

4. Fold the rectangle into an accordion, which will be the dragon's body.

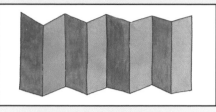

5. Glue or tape the head to one end of the dragon's body. Glue or tape the tail to the other end.

6. Tape one of the popsicle sticks to the head and the other to the tail, so you can hold on to your dragon and make it move or dance.

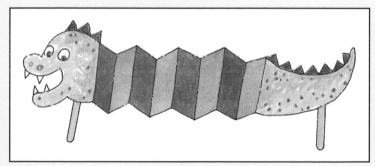

Word List

Challenging Words	parade		
Long A Decodable Words	braid brave cape day Drake face Gabe	Gail hair Jade Kate mane mare nails	paint say shades tail wave
High-Frequency Words	a all am and are at be black blue colors come does gives	going great has her his I in is it long looks me	of on see she so stop the they three to very